Grandma Marian mixes fact and fancy. You will enjoy the adventures of this friendly giraffe while learning about his habitat, his instincts and even his enemies.

What they're saying about Grandma Marian's Books:

"..the poetic and informative text flows smoothly as it captivates and educates young audiences. I highly recommend the acquisition of Grandma Marian's books to all collectors of books for children."
>--Myra S. Zoll
>Maumee Valley Country Day School

"..a rare gift of narrative ability."
>--Rosemary Stephens
>The Penwoman

"My grandchildern love Grandma Marian's books and so do I!"
>--Al Hirt

"Grandma Marian's books are informative and entertaining for children of all ages."
>--Vantage

"...fun as well as informative, clear and well thought out, all of which are very important for learning."
>--Devon Davis, Special Ed. teacher
>Center School,
>National Institute of Dislexia

"Grandma Marian has a wonderful gift of teaching interesting and important facts about animals with entertaining rhymes. My kids love 'em and yours will too!"
>--Gary Burghoff
>Emmy winning actor of MASH

"Grandma Marian's books capture young hearts"
>--Barbara Mann, The Jewish Standard
>Toronto, Canada

First Edition
Second Printing, 1989

Text Copyright © by Marian Goldner
Illustration: Copyright © by Donna Sott
Library of Congress Catalog Card Number 85-71331

ISBN 0-9614989-0-0

Georgie the Jovial Giraffe

by Grandma Marian

For Grandpa Leo

Published by Banmar, Inc.

New York   South Carolina

Printed in Hungary

Illustrated by Donna Sott

I once knew a creature who just loved to laugh--
A tall gangly fellow known as Georgie Giraffe.

Now Georgie was different
From chaps of his kind
Who stayed by themselves
When they wandered and dined.

In African heat,
Among grasslands and trees,
He would look for a friend
To play games with or tease.

While others were eating
Sweet leaves way up high,
Old George would trot up,
Bump their necks and then cry,

"How 'bout a race
To the desert and back?"
They'd just roll their big eyes
And continue to snack.

He found sweet mimosa, acacia leaves too,
Which he gave to the others, then just watched them chew.

He just wouldn't give up,
He was really warm hearted,
Always trying new ways
To get friendship started.

For he liked being friendly
And he meant them no harm,
But they just didn't care much
For his kind of charm.

After while, some giraffes did come closer to hear
This jovial Georgie spreading good cheer.

Now, strange as it seems,
I'll tell you right now,
When giraffes make a noise
They sound much like a cow!

Their voice box, you see,
Is quite small for their size,
So they don't chatter much,
Which is probably wise.

Poor Georgie's remarks were like moos, grunts and groans,
But giraffes understood, and it tickled their bones.

Where giraffes live, you know,
It is sandy and dry.
Sometimes between drinks
Many weeks can go by!

They can get lots of water
From plants that they eat,
But giraffes never never
Eat any meat.

Well, one sunny day
In the spring of the year
Georgie's sharp eyes
Saw a dust cloud appear.

Driving winds came along blowing sand. What a sight!
But giraffes never care; they just close their nose tight!

As the sand storm diminished, something else came to view--
Two or three jeeps and a camera crew.

Old George and his friends saw the men coming near,
But they kept right on eating without any fear.

The men took their pictures
With shouts of delight,
Admiring these creatures
Of beauty and height.

Georgie came nearer, his long slim neck swaying,
Thinking it was a nice game they were playing.

Approaching the cameras, he blinked his long lashes
And poked out his tongue at the sudden light flashes.

The photographers laughed at this friendly display
And took pictures galore of giraffes the whole day.

Then, when it was mealtime
The men shared their fruit
With George and his friends,
But it caused a dispute.

One critter was selfish
And started to bite,
Though giraffes hardly ever
Get ornery and fight.

But he soon became calm
When he looked through the trees
And saw that strange Georgie
Get down on his knees!

As each man approached
George would kneel nice and low.

**Then the man would mount up
And away George would go!**

Soon other giraffes joined the fun giving rides,
Or they'd sit on their haunches so their backs became slides!

The men held on tight, for his back is slantwise
From his neck to his tail, with which he swats flies!

Such fun they all had that wonderful day!
The giraffes, they felt sad when the men went away.

But Georgie said, "Hey! Stick with me, everyone!
If we stay together, we can always have fun!

In the evening, as Georgie looked off once again,
He saw a big lion come out of his den!

George mood just as loud
As his voice box would go,
For his friends were in danger,
And they didn't know!

He leaped through the tall grass to spread the alarm.
Soon all the giraffes were fleeing from harm.

What a sight to the eyes, I shall never forget,
As they gracefully galloped toward the golden sunset.

Their tall, spindly legs moved in rhythm and style.
With a long, swinging stride they ran mile after mile.

When the last giraffe fled,
Georgie stopped in his track,
For that lion was ready
To pounce on his back!

His mane flying wild, the lion leaped high,
Just as Georgie's hind hoofs thumped above his left eye!

The king of the beasts was knocked out with one blow!
I saw the whole thing and that's how I know.

Then Georgie lunged off
In a swiftly paced gait.
He had saved all his friends
From a horrible fate.

Now, giraffes stay together--
That is, more or less,
For they all bear in mind
Georgie's rule for success:

"Though we cannot talk much,
We should travel in herds,
Then our friendly good deeds
Will speak louder than words!"

Other books by Grandma Marian:

BENI THE BASHFUL BEAVER

I MET A GIANT PANDA

MRS. PAM POLAR BEAR